Camilla
the Cupcake Fairy

Tim Bugbird • Lara Ede

make
believe
ideas

On **Camilla's** fifth birthday,

the Pink Fairy Post

sent to Camilla what she

dreamed of most.

Not a **hat,** or a **doll,** or a **plant** in a pot,

or anything else she'd already got.

fairy garden

She tore off the paper and giggled with glee.

"A wand!" cried Camilla.

"And meant just for me!"

It was ever so shiny and sparkly and new.
Her very first wand! But **what** would it do?

If she **waved** it quite **carefully**
and closed her eyes **tight,**

could she wish for a party with dancing all night?

Or if she sat nicely,
not making a noise,
would it make her bed neatly
and tidy her toys?

Or would it put on a **show** with a **dancing** dog,

The answer was **no!**
But what it would make,
Camilla was told, was
frosting for cake!
So she found a plain **cupcake**,
which she placed by her feet,
her **wand** at the ready,
to make a pink treat!

And holding the **wand**, Camilla stood straight.

She took a deep breath but just **could** **not** **wait** . . .

She waved it so fast,

the wand would not stop

whirling and twirling

and flashing on top!

It jumped and it jerked,

with a rattle and a shake,

it jiggled and it juddered

'til she thought

it would break!

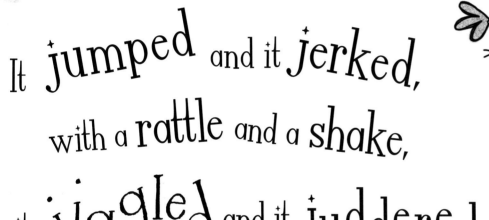

Then, with a BANG,

bright stars filled the air.

She looked for

sweet frosting,

but the cupcake was bare!

And there on the top,

not making a sound,

was a tiny white

mouse,

with eyes bright

and round!

So she started again, this time taking care
to wave the wand gently. But look what was there!

Covering the cake where

the frosting should be . . .

fluffy potato was all she could see!

So she tried one more wave, not too fast or too slow.

Now topping the cake there was nothing but . . .

snow!

Well, **snowballs** and **snowmen**
she didn't much mind,
but this *fancy frosting*
was quite the
wrong kind!

"Oh dear," thought Camilla.
"This just isn't right.
My wand is not working,
I'll be here all night!"

But then, when it seemed she was down on her luck,

Miss Sprinkles drove by in her pink fairy truck.

Camilla asked nicely, "Miss, what should I do?"

Her teacher said kindly, "I'll give you a clue!"

"Working alone is never much fun,
but with help from your friends, the job is soon done!"

So she called her **friends** on her pink fairy phone.

Molly and Maya were glad to be home.

Said Molly to Maya,
"Our friend's in a state!
Let's fly to Camilla,
this problem
won't wait!"

They held the wand steady
with eyes closed tight.
As they worked hard together,
it shone a bright light.

Then crossing their fingers
in a shower of gold twinkles,
they all wished together
for frosting and
sprinkles!

All of a sudden,
the fairy friends found
the tastiest treat,
just there on the ground.
With sparkling
sprinkles
and frosting
so sweet,

the best-ever
cupcake
was right at their feet!